Nobody's Perfect

A Story for Children About Perfectionism

by Ellen Flanagan Burns
illustrated by Erica Pelton Villnave

MAGINATION PRESS • WASHINGTON D.C.

For my family, Brian and Kaelyn - EFB

For Carol, Gretchen, Julie, Kristen, and Kyra - EPV

Published by

MAGINATION PRESS
An Educational Publishing Foundation Book
American Psychological Association
750 First Street, NE
Washington, DC 20002

For more information about our books, including a complete catalog, please write to us, call 1-800-374-2721, or visit our website at www.maginationpress.com.

Printed by Phoenix Color, Hagerstown, Maryland

Library of Congress Cataloging-in-Publication Data

Burns, Ellen Flanagan.
Nobody's perfect : a story for children about perfectionism / by Ellen Flanagan Burns ; illustrated by Erica Pelton Villnave.
p. cm.
Summary: Sally overcomes her perfectionism when her teachers and mother help her realize that making mistakes is a part of learning, and that doing her best is good enough.
ISBN-13: 978-1-4338-0379-6 (hardcover : alk. paper)
ISBN-10: 1-4338-0379-8 (hardcover : alk. paper)
ISBN-13: 978-1-4338-0380-2 (pbk. : alk. paper)
ISBN-10: 1-4338-0380-1 (pbk. : alk. paper)
[1. Perfectionism (Personality trait)—Fiction.] I. Villnave, Erica Pelton, ill. II. Title. III. Title: Nobody's perfect.
PZ7.B9366No 2008
[Fic]—dc22   2008017619

10 9 8 7

Table of Contents

Dear Reader

Have you ever dreamed of having the perfect family and friends, getting straight A's, being the best player on the team, or being the smartest, best looking, most talented? Most of us have wanted to be the best from time to time. But if you've ever tried to be perfect like Sally Sanders, you've probably discovered that it's not all it seems.

Trying to be the best at everything makes Sally cranky and nervous. After all, you feel a lot of pressure when you try to make yourself perfect! Making an awesome project in school, getting the lead part in the play, being the most talented musician. It's exhausting! Sally is so busy trying to be the best and working hard to please everyone else that she forgets to have fun. Sometimes she's afraid of doing something wrong, so she doesn't do anything at all! She believes people might think she's not so special after all and won't like her. She just doesn't feel free to be herself.

After a while, Sally discovers that mistakes aren't as embarrassing or as awful as she thought. Even though it's no fun to make mistakes, it's okay—you can even learn from them. Breaking a glass, putting too much salt in the cookie batter, or not being a very good basketball player. It stinks sometimes, but "that's life," as Sally's drama teacher says. Sometimes mistakes have a purpose. They show us what we need to do differently and they help us grow. And all of our little quirks make us more loveable. Thank goodness for our friend who can wiggle her ears (it makes everyone laugh), or our hair that won't curl (but is shiny), or our mom's funny laugh that's contagious. It's part of what makes us…us!

With a little help, Sally realizes she's doesn't have to be the best at everything, instead she can be her best in some things, the things she really likes. She discovers there are better reasons for doing things like making new friends, having fun, and learning new things.

If you find yourself thinking like Sally did, you can change your mind, too. Give yourself permission to try new things just for fun, and when you make mistakes, keep going. When you find something you enjoy, you'll get better with patience and practice but most of all you'll have fun. Happiness comes with enjoying yourself, from doing your best, and from knowing you're good enough just the way you are.

Your *(former, slightly perfectionist)* friend,
Ellen

About the Author

ELLEN FLANAGAN BURNS, a school psychologist and licensed massage therapist, has dealt with perfectionism personally and professionally, and she has worked with many children suffering from anxiety. She believes that children's books can be a powerful therapeutic tool and is a strong supporter of holistic and cognitive-based interventions for children with anxiety-related issues. Ms. Burns lives in Newark, Delaware with her family.

About the Illustrator

ERICA PELTON VILLNAVE's involvement in children's literature began at the Maryland Institute College of Art where she studied illustration. Her watercolor illustrations are filled with whimsical imagery, vibrant colors and details that can guide both child and adult along wonderful journeys to any place and time. An animated cast of characters share the variety of experiences and emotions in the life of every child. Such images, of characters and situations, give voice and vision to the stories as they are read and experienced by each child.

Chapter 1

The Recital

"Sally Sanders is next," announced Mrs. Pratt. Sally walked to the front of the living room and sat at the piano. She glanced around and saw her mom, dad and little brother, Billy, and the parents of Mrs. Pratt's other students, all sitting in mismatched chairs gathered from around her teacher's house. It was Sally's turn to play at the recital, her turn to shine bright like a star, and she looked forward to it.

She began her first piece, "Ocean Waves," playing softly at first, then much harder, just like real waves that slowly build then forcefully crash onto a sandy beach.

Sally memorized the piece even though Mrs. Pratt said she could use her book because she didn't want to take the easy way out. Besides, she wanted to play like the older students and they usually memorized their pieces. Next she performed "Clowns at the Circus" lightly and quickly, the way silly clowns juggle for a crowd. As she neared the end of the piece, her finger slipped onto a wrong key and the sounds clashed. To Sally, it felt like the whole piece was ruined, like her whole performance was a flop. She was embarrassed and mad, all at the same time, which is an awful mix. Probably as awful as an onion and garlic milkshake tastes, if you can imagine. Sally wanted to shrink down to the size of a worm and hide under the pedals of the piano.

She sat by her family when she was done, feeling relieved to hear Mrs. Pratt announcing the next student.

"Very good!" Mr. Sanders whispered. Her mom agreed.

Sally didn't. "I ruined everything," was all she could think. She looked around the room at the other students and felt like she didn't belong there — she spoiled the group. She decided she would have to practice even more every day just to be as good as everyone else. "After all, accomplished players didn't make mistakes," she thought.

Afterwards, Mrs. Pratt invited everyone to the kitchen for refreshments. In the middle of the kitchen table, surrounded by plates of chocolate chip cookies and crackers, was a big bowl of peach punch. Floating in the punch were scoops of vanilla ice cream and ice cubes in the shape of a quarter note.

Sally didn't feel like talking to anyone. And she was pretty sure there wasn't anyone who wanted to talk to her either. "Nobody wants to hang around with a loser," she told herself. She took a sip of punch and stood by herself.

Jill walked over and stood next to Sally. She played right before Sally in the recital. "I liked your pieces," Jill said.

Sally said, "But I messed up on the second one. It sounded really bad."

"Oh, I didn't notice," Jill said. She shrugged, "I made a couple of mistakes too. It's no big deal."

Sally thought Jill was just trying to be nice. She couldn't remember Jill ever making a mistake when she played. In

fact, she made it look so easy all the time.

After another sip of punch and a chocolate chip cookie, Sally was ready to leave.

She wasn't in a very good mood and most of all she didn't want to face Mrs. Pratt. Sally felt like she had let her down.

Chapter 2

All or Nothing

"Settle down everyone. Please have a seat!" Ms. Sharp told the students the next day at school. There was a buzz of excitement in the air as the students hustled into the classroom, eager to hear what role they landed after last week's auditions for *Grease*, the school's spring play.

"Quiet please," Ms. Sharp said again, over the noise. Ms. Sharp was their drama teacher and the director of the show. She had fiery red hair and frizzy curls that had a mind of their own. She was usually able to wrestle it all into a messy bun on the top of her head, where she often stuck a pencil or two. By the end of the day though, one or two curls usually escaped and bounced in front of her eyes. But Ms. Sharp looked great!

Most students loved drama class. Ms. Sharp had a way of bringing out the best in everyone, probably because it was okay to make mistakes with her; it was accepted, even expected. Ms. Sharp believed that mistakes were a part of life. She said Albert Einstein and Eleanor Roosevelt both admitted making plenty of mistakes on their way to greatness and afterwards, too. So no one held back in drama class. And when someone made a mistake, like when Steven forgot his lines and Julie got the giggles or when Sarah could only act like a nice witch instead of a mean one, Ms. Sharp would say it was okay. That's life. It became a classroom joke after awhile and before they knew it, some kids could even laugh at their own mistakes. But Sally Sanders wasn't one of those kids.

Ms. Sharp knew a lot about plays because she was an actress and a director with the local theater. "I've posted this year's cast list on the bulletin board in the hallway," she announced. "After class, you are welcome to go take a look. I want to thank each of you for trying out. I think it's going to be a great show."

Nobody wanted to wait until the end of class to check out the bulletin board. A few groans and moans of disappointment could be heard over her voice.

Sally was hoping to land the lead role of "Sandy," because she thought it was the most important role in the whole show. Earlier that year, she saw the play on Broadway with her family and "Sandy" made everything look so easy and effortless. Sally wanted to do the same thing.

Class seemed to last twice as long that day. When it was finally over, a group of students dashed to the bulletin board. Some were pushing and squirming to get close to the cast list and that made it almost impossible for everyone else to see. Sally stood on her tiptoes so she could see over their heads. Once her eyes finally found "Sandy" she followed the line across the page. "Oh, no!" She read Jane's name instead of hers. Pamela was listed as Jane's understudy. Sally's name was listed as only the piano player.

"Congratulations, Jane," Sally said. But deep down Sally felt like a big loser. She didn't even get a part in the play. How could this be? She wondered what Jane had that she didn't have. "I wish I were more like Jane," she thought.

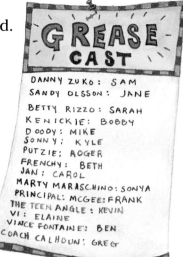

GREASE CAST

DANNY ZUKO: SAM
SANDY OLSSON: JANE
BETTY RIZZO: SARAH
KENICKIE: BOBBY
DOODY: MIKE
SONNY: KYLE
PUTZIE: ROGER
FRENCHY: BETH
JAN: CAROL
MARTY MARASCHINO: SONYA
PRINCIPAL: MCGEE: FRANK
THE TEEN ANGLE: KEVIN
VI: ELAINE
VINCE FONTAINE: BEN
COACH CALHOUN: GREG

Sally's best friend Jenny tugged at her arm. "Sally you're the piano player! That's awesome!"

"But I'm not 'Sandy.' I don't even have a real part," Sally groaned. She knew if she had done a better job at auditions, she would have gotten it. "I should've practiced more," she said.

"That's okay, I didn't get a part, either," Jenny said. "I'm working on scenery." Jenny was excited because she had a flair for drawing. She loved it.

"What's the point?" Sally grumbled. "If you're not the lead or at least one of the main characters, then nobody cares about you. I don't want to be in this dumb play anymore. What about you?" she asked.

Jenny shook her head at Sally. She talked to Sally about all the fun she couldn't wait to have with the backstage crew. She was excited about doing her part. "Come on, we're going to have so much fun!" she said with a big smile.

Sally couldn't understand why Jenny thought they would have fun. After all, making scenery and playing the piano weren't very important parts of the show. They wouldn't be stars. No one would notice them. She walked to her next class alone, leaving Jenny standing and talking with the other kids.

Chapter 3

Winners and Losers

Mr. Slip was setting up the volleyball net in the gym just as Sally's class entered. "Girls against boys!" he cried out to the delight of the whole class. Yes! The gym erupted with cheers.

Sally and the other girls rallied around in a circle to get psyched. The boys high-fived each other. Sally was glad because she was a good volleyball player. "This is our chance to show the boys we're better than they are," she told the girls.

But it wasn't long before the boys had a six-point lead. Josh served the ball to Nancy, but she wasn't able to get to it quickly enough and the girls lost another point.

"Come on Nancy! Don't just stand there, bend your knees and get the ball!" Sally yelled with frustration. "We have to win!"

Nancy's face turned red with embarrassment. Sally's yelling made it seem like she did something wrong or something bad on purpose. Now it felt like all that mattered was winning, and Nancy wasn't having as much fun anymore.

When it was Pam's turn to serve, the girls started

catching up and Sally started feeling happy again. Then the ball went to Samantha and Jane, but each one thought the other would get it and it landed on the floor between them. The girls lost the point, but they giggled at their mistake. Sally was fuming. They were giving away points for free! She thought her teammates weren't even trying and, to make matters worse, they didn't seem to care. "Come on you guys, you have to pay attention!" she snapped. Jane and Samantha looked at each other and rolled their eyes.

The boys served the next round and spiked the ball to Jenny, who hit the ball out of bounds. Sally was losing hope. She pulled her team together for a quick pep talk and some pointers to help them. She told everyone to keep the ball away from the good players on the boys' team. "It's our only chance!" Sally pleaded.

"Sally, don't worry so much, it's just a game," Jenny reminded her.

"What?!" Sally thought. "It's always important to win."

When they lost the game, Sally thought her teammates were losers for not playing hard enough and she felt doubly angry to be on the losing side. "I hope we never play girls against boys again," she told Jenny.

Afterwards, on their way back to class, Jenny pointed to a poster in the hallway, her eyes as big as saucers. "Look Sally, soccer sign-ups are this week!" she said. Jenny had looked forward to playing with the Tigers all year. Sally thought it would be fun to play, too, but she wondered if she would be good enough for the team. She'd never played soccer. "I don't want to make a fool of myself," she thought nervously. "Jenny, are you *sure* you want to play?" she asked.

"Of course! We've been talking about this all year!" Jenny said enthusiastically, smiling from ear to ear. "It will be fun."

"I'll have to think about it some more," Sally said. She liked trying new things about as much as a cat liked going for a swim unless she knew she'd be good. She didn't have that feeling now. "I might not be any good," she told Jenny.

"So?" Jenny said. "I might not be any good either. It's no big deal."

How could she say that? Of course it was a big deal. Being bad at something would be embarrassing and nothing was worth taking that chance. "The Tigers are probably a really good team," she warned Jenny.

"Don't worry, the poster says beginners are welcomed." Jenny said. "So I'm sure we'll be good enough." But Sally didn't want to be just good enough—she wanted to be better than that.

"I don't know," she said, "I don't think I'm going to play."

"Jeez, Sally. Do you have to be the best at everything?"

"Well nobody wants to be a loser," Sally snapped. She thought Jenny would surely understand that.

"I just like having fun with you, Sally," Jenny said, "and even if you weren't very good, you would never be a loser."

Sally didn't know what to say. She liked having fun with her friend, too.

Jenny's smile faded as they walked the rest of the way in silence.

Chapter 4

Getting A's

Mrs. Watson divided the class into small groups for their next science project, a diorama of ocean life. She was Sally's favorite teacher because she was so nice and always full of good ideas. "And see if you can make it fit it into a shoebox!" Mrs. Watson added.

Sally partnered with Karen and Oliver. She came prepared with ideas for making the best project ever. "I saw a diorama in a museum once that used magnets to move the objects around," she said. "And instead of one shoebox we should use a bunch and layer them to show all of the levels of the ocean."

"That's really cool Sally, but trust me, we'll never finish on time!" Oliver said.

"Yeah, those are great ideas, but Oliver's right; it's too much," Karen said. "We could do some of it, but I don't think Mrs. Watson expects us to do it all." If they followed all of Sally's suggestions, they would have their work cut out for them. And even though Oliver and Karen were good students, they didn't think all that effort was necessary. Besides they had other things to do, too.

Sally felt frustrated and a little hurt that they weren't as excited about her ideas as she was.

Karen shared her idea of dividing the project into smaller parts to make it easier to handle. She offered to make the background scenes with paint and modeling clay, and because Oliver liked to write, she thought he could be in charge of writing a description of the diorama. "Sally, you're so creative, you could make all of the sea life creatures," Karen suggested. "When we're done, we can put it all together."

"But it's going to be the same as everyone else's project!" Sally objected. She felt annoyed that Karen and Oliver weren't coming up with better ideas, something more creative and original. It seemed like they were taking the easy way out. And Oliver could easily ruin their project, she worried, because after all, "he isn't a very good writer," she told herself. She was also afraid Karen wouldn't put much effort into her part. "She doesn't care about her work as much as I do," she thought.

Sally pushed her ideas again, hoping to motivate Karen and Oliver. "We can make it happen!" she promised. "I'm going to work on it all weekend, just come over and help when you can," she said. "I really don't mind doing most of it myself." Sally would rather do it all than take the chance that her friends would do something wrong. For her, the only way to do something right was to do it herself.

Because Sally was famous for her elaborate projects and straight A's, Karen and Oliver didn't want to stand in her way. They knew it was Sally's way or no way, and it didn't really matter if they were on board or not. The project was still going forward as Sally wanted.

"I have some things to do this Saturday, but I'll be over when I'm done," Karen offered.

Oliver remembered a baseball game he was playing in that same day. "I'll be over after the game," he said.

"That's okay," Sally said. She assured them, "We'll all get A's, you'll see!"

Sally knew she had a long weekend of work ahead of her and there wouldn't be any time for fun. But she was used to that. And it would all be worthwhile once Mrs. Watson saw their project, she told herself.

Karen and Oliver looked at each other and shrugged. They didn't know what else to do.

Chapter 5

Out of Time!

Sally prided herself on being one of the top students in her class. She had the ribbons and trophies to show for it.

"4TH GRADE MATH WHIZ"

"5TH GRADE SPELLING BEE CHAMPION"

"HONOR ROLL ~ 5 YEARS"

"1ST PLACE ~ SCIENCE FAIR"

"YOUNG MUSICIANS CONTEST WINNER"

She kept them safe on a shelf in her bedroom. But Sally still felt uneasy about some of the projects her classmates made with their new computer programs. It's not that they weren't good enough, it was just the opposite. They were great, even better than hers. Kaelyn and Brian used lots of eye-popping design and flashy detail in their projects. Everyone seemed impressed with them and told them how awesome they were. One time Kaelyn put together a multi-media presentation on global warming when all they had to do was make a poster. "That was really annoying! And totally unfair!" Sally thought. But she wished she could do the same thing. Sally tried to make her own projects better, but it was next to impossible since she didn't have the right tools. It was hopeless.

A few weeks after Sally handed in the diorama (they got an A, thanks to Sally's weekend of work and a little help from Karen and Oliver), Sally was having a hard time finishing an assignment that was due tomorrow. Not only was it not finished, she hadn't even started. Her teacher, Mrs. Watson, told the class to find some interesting facts about the geography of any country in the world. But a list

of facts seemed boring to Sally. She thought about building a sculpture of Italy to show its boot shape or writing a report on Africa's rainforest. "It would be cool to bring in my pictures from Spain, but that's too easy." Lots of ideas whirled around Sally's head. Yet nothing seemed good enough to her and time was running out. She wondered what Kaelyn and Brian were doing. She figured it would be really cool, whatever it was. Sally felt tired and grumpy. "I should've started sooner," she told herself. She thought she needed at least another week to get it done right. After a while, she just couldn't think about the project anymore, so she decided not to make one at all. Besides, she thought, whatever she did wouldn't be good enough anyway.

Chapter 6

The Perfect Puppy

At school the next day, Mrs. Watson collected everyone's project. Almost everyone handed one in except for some kids who came ready with excuses. "Computer crashed, sorry!" Sam yelled from the back of the room. "My pet iguana ate it!" Pam added wryly, as the class burst out laughing.

"Bring them tomorrow!" Mrs. Watson said. "Better late than never." Then Mrs. Watson noticed Sally's project was missing, too. "Sally, where's your project?" Some of Sally's classmates' jaws dropped when they saw Sally hadn't brought it in.

Sally looked embarrassed and shrugged. "I just couldn't decide what to do," she explained, feeling butterflies in her stomach, "and then I ran out of time." She shared some of her ideas with Mrs. Watson.

"Those are terrific ideas for bigger projects. This time, think short and sweet," Mrs. Watson suggested.

Sally searched for an idea but still couldn't decide on one. It was really hard for her to think short and sweet. She always wanted to think bigger and better.

Mrs. Watson saw that Sally was still struggling. "This

BARK! BARK!

reminds me of a story about a boy who wanted a puppy," Mrs. Watson said. "He searched high and low for the perfect one. Some puppies had floppy ears or brown spots, others barked too much and most of them wanted to chew on his shoes. Since they weren't perfect, he kept right on searching."

"A perfect puppy? There's no such thing!" Sally said. "Everyone knows puppies are just right the way they are."

Mrs. Watson agreed. "I wouldn't change a thing about my puppy. But things will be easier once he's potty-trained. And you're right, the boy never found a perfect puppy, but he finally found one he wanted. It had a black ear and a white ear and oodles of curls all over."

"Sounds just

right!" Sally replied. She thought about it. "But a puppy isn't a project."

"True, but there's no such thing as a perfect anything," Mrs. Watson gently reminded her. "So choose a project that interests you, and it will be just right too because it will be just right for you."

"My pictures from Spain, I guess" Sally said. She felt relieved to have decided on the project and it felt good.

"Wonderful!" Mrs. Watson said. "Bring them tomorrow."

Chapter 7

The Weary Baker

Sally walked to her piano lesson after school. It had been a week since the recital. She still wondered if Mrs. Pratt was as disappointed in her as she was in herself for ruining everything. Sally felt butterflies in her stomach for the second time that day as she rang the doorbell.

"Come in, Sally," Mrs. Pratt said as she opened the door. She was wearing an oven mitt. "I just finished baking a batch of cookies." The smell of sugar cookies wafted past Sally as she walked in. "Care for some?" she asked.

"Thank you," Sally said. She sat at the piano with a plate of cookies and a glass of milk. "Sorry about the recital." A tear gathered on her lower eyelid.

"No worries," Mrs. Pratt said. "Mistakes are a normal part of things. Everyone makes them."

Sally was surprised to hear Mrs. Pratt say that.

"Even the best players make mistakes from time to time," added Mrs. Pratt, "and do you know what they do?"

Sally shook her head.

"They keep right on playing," Mrs. Pratt said. "You know, this reminds me of a story my piano teacher told me when I was your age. Want to hear it?"

Sally nodded.

"It's about a baker who made lots of tasty treats. People loved his buttery cookies, his fancy pies, and moist cakes. He even won the award three years in a row for the best strawberry strudel. Only the best was good enough for the baker. When a cheesecake turned out light and fluffy the way he liked it or a piecrust was flaky and golden brown, he felt a flash of satisfaction. But when he made a mistake (which happened every day), like when a gingerbread man's button was slightly burned, or a brownie had too many chocolate chips, it went straight into the garbage! Over time the baker grew weary of it all, he felt tired and grumpy and wasn't having fun anymore.

"One day a lady walked in. She couldn't decide what to order, so she asked the baker what he liked best. The baker had no idea; unfortunately, he never had enough time to

taste anything. He was too busy for that. He even forgot what his jellyrolls tasted like!

"'I don't know, but the strawberry strudels are a big hit,' he said to the lady.

"That night after the bakery closed and it was time to sweep up, the baker nibbled some of his cakes and pies and sweet icings, too. I think he was curious. Ah, the rich chocolates, creamy custards, and buttery pastries! The combination of flavors, filled him with joy and satisfaction, and he remembered why he loved to bake. He felt light and happy for the first time in years and began dancing with the broom around the bakery. From then on, he never threw away another gingerbread man with a slightly burned button or brownie with too many chocolate chips. They were too tasty! Instead, he put them out for his customers to enjoy, right next to free samples of his favorite pastries. People came from all over just to try them and his business grew and grew."

"The baker started having fun again," Sally noticed with a reluctant smile, "mistakes and all." But she still cringed when she thought of her mistake at the recital.

Chapter 8

Stars of the Show

Rehearsals for *Grease* were fast approaching. Sally decided she was not going to just be the piano player, and she needed to tell Ms. Sharp that she wouldn't be in the show.

Ms. Sharp looked up from her papers when she heard a knock at the door. She was surprised to see Sally poking her head into the classroom. "Come in!" Ms. Sharp said. "You're early. Rehearsals don't start for another week."

"I know," Sally said. "I need to tell you something."

Ms. Sharp asked what was on her mind as she stuck another pencil in her hair.

"Um…the play," Sally said, "I'm not going to be in it."

"That's too bad. It won't be the same without you, Sally. Do you have other plans that day?" Ms. Sharp asked.

"No. It's just that…I wanted to be 'Sandy.' I wanted to be the star of the show, and the piano player is practically invisible," Sally explained. "Now there's no point in being in it."

"Oh, I understand," Ms. Sharp said with a knowing look in her eyes. "Getting the lead can be exciting for some people, but other roles are fun, too."

"But the star is the most important role in the whole show," Sally said.

Ms. Sharp understood how Sally felt. "The star of the show does get a lot of attention, and the actors are important. But there's a lot more to it. A great show also needs beautiful scenery to make the setting more interesting and realistic. That takes hard work and a whole lot of creativity and artistic flair, the kind that Pam and Jenny have," Ms. Sharp said.

Sally agreed. They were just right for the job because they were imaginative and crafty.

"And a good show needs strong and dependable stagehands to move the scenery around and put everything in its place. I thought Sarah and Peter would be just right for that job. And I need someone who can pay close attention in order to shine the lights at the right time, on the right people,  someone who can figure out how to work all those tricky buttons and switches. Eric, of course."

Sally nodded. Everyone knew that Eric was really good with gadgets and super smart, too, and Sarah and Peter were dependable.

"And every play needs people who can work well together to write a good script, which is why Tom and Mary got the job," Ms. Sharp when on.

Sally knew Tom and Mary were cooperative and both of them liked to write.

"And every musical needs melodies with a harmony and beat to bring it to life," Ms. Sharp said. "That's why I chose you to be the piano player.

Sally could see that everyone had an important job to do, something special to offer. That was fine for them, but she still wanted the lead role. Even so, she thought she might give the idea a chance.

She talked it out with Ms. Sharp. "Plays are sort of like puzzles," Sally said.

"Yes, I guess they are," Ms. Sharp agreed. "And everyone has a piece."

"Yeah," said Sally, thinking aloud, "and every piece makes the whole thing a little more complete."

Ms. Sharp agreed as a curl bounced onto her forehead. "If I had to choose between the actors and the artists, I'd be in trouble," Ms. Sharp went on.

"Yeah, there wouldn't be any action without the actors and it would be pretty dull without the artists," Sally agreed.

"And where would our play be without a director or lights?"

"Pretty disorganized…and dark."

"And where would our play be without a piano player?" Ms. Sharp finally asked.

"It would be a pretty quiet play," conceded Sally.

Sally thanked Ms. Sharp and went into the hallway to think some more. Maybe Jane wasn't better than she was, maybe she was just better for that role, just as Sally was better for playing the piano. Maybe… Sally started to think she might have fun doing her part after all.

After thinking it over for a while, Sally decided to change her mind about being in the play, but she wondered if it was too late. "Ms. Sharp," she asked as she peeked into the classroom, "is it okay if I take back the part of the piano player?"

"I wouldn't have it any other way. And there will be other plays and other roles," she gently reminded Sally.

Sally realized there would

be new opportunities for stardom in the future. But for now, she would be the piano player and for the first time, she felt excited about doing her part in the play. And even though she wouldn't be the lead this time, she felt happy to have an important part in the play.

"Did you ever get the lead role?" Sally asked her teacher.

"On occasion," Ms. Sharp said. "But there was a girl I used to know who missed out on a lot of fun roles because she felt the same way you used to feel."

Sally noticed a twinkle in her teacher's eye.

"Ms. Sharp, was it you?" she asked.

Ms. Sharp winked and smiled at Sally. "See you at rehearsals, Sally."

Chapter 9

Good Enough

When Sally got home from school, she saw her mom painting in the backyard. Her brother Billy was playing basketball nearby. She dropped her books on the kitchen table and raced out to see them.

"Guess what," she said, plopping down in the grass next to her mom.

"Let me guess, another A?" her brother teased. Mrs. Sanders looked disapprovingly toward Billy.

"Very funny. It's time for soccer sign-ups," Sally said.

"That's good news!" Mrs. Sanders said. "Soccer sounds like fun."

Sally nodded and watched her mom paint their tulip garden with purple and pink watercolors. She wanted to tell her what happened with Jenny in the hallway and her feelings about soccer but didn't know how.

"You like painting, huh," she said instead.

Mrs. Sanders nodded. "I feel happy when I paint. I guess you could say painting's my thing."

"Probably because you're so good at it," Sally replied.

"Thanks. That helps, but it's not really why I like painting and it certainly doesn't explain why I like playing

tennis too," Mrs. Sanders pointed out.

"Yeah, because you always lose!" Billy called out after shooting a basket.

"That's okay, losing doesn't make me a loser," Mrs. Sanders called back. "Imagine all the fun I'd miss if I let that stop me. Besides, I'm getting better and enjoying myself more all the time."

After painting another tulip, Mrs. Sanders asked, "Did you sign up for soccer?"

"No, but Jenny did," Sally replied.

"Oh. Don't you want to play?" Mrs. Sanders asked.

Sally shrugged. "If I played I wouldn't have as much time for homework," she pointed out.

"Your schoolwork is important," Mrs. Sanders said, putting down her paintbrush, "and I'm proud of you for working hard. But there's something that's just as important as working hard…"

"Getting good grades, probably," Sally thought to herself.

"…having fun," Mrs. Sanders said.

Sally was surprised to hear her mom say that it was important to work hard *and* have fun.

"If I didn't make time for painting and playing tennis,

I wouldn't be very happy," Mrs. Sanders said.

"But I might not be any good at soccer," Sally added. It was the real reason she didn't sign up. She felt embarrassed to admit that she might not be good at something. After all, she was used to being the best at most things she did.

"That's okay," Mrs. Sanders assured her. "Imagine all the fun you'll miss if you let that stop you."

But Sally wasn't so sure. "I wouldn't have any fun if I wasn't good and didn't win," said Sally with a huff.

"Why not?" her mother asked.

"You don't get it," she sighed, "because you would never paint a bad picture."

"It wasn't always that way," Mrs. Sanders replied.

"Come with me." She went inside and dug out some of her old paintings.

"No way!" Sally said. She was surprised by how different they looked and that some of them weren't very good.

"Way!" Mrs. Sanders laughed. "Nobody was breaking down the doors to buy these, but it didn't matter to me."

"Why did you stick with it?" Sally asked. Sally couldn't believe her mom continued to paint when she wasn't very good at it. She thought that was really brave.

"Because I was learning. I love mixing colors together and creating pictures. For me, painting is relaxing and fun all at the same time. And being good at it is just like icing on the cake." Mrs. Sanders explained.

Sally could see how much her mom loved painting. "So soccer could be my thing if I like it," Sally realized.

"Sure," Mrs. Sanders agreed.

"And I might get better, too," Sally added.

"Sure, with patience and practice. But for now you'll be learning something new and making new friends, too," Mrs. Sanders said. "And those are pretty good reasons to give it a try, don't you think?"

"But what if I don't like it?"

"Then it won't be your thing. You'll find something else. But you won't know if you like soccer until you try it for a little while."

After thinking it over, there was something Sally wanted to know. "Would you be upset if I wasn't very good?" she asked because most of all, Sally worried about disappointing her mom and dad.

"No, not at all," said Mrs. Sanders as she hugged Sally. "Where did that idea come from?"

Sally shrugged. She wasn't sure.

"Sally, you don't have to be a soccer champ or a straight A student to please me or your dad," Mrs. Sanders said. "After all, we love you just the way you are."

Sally was trying to wrap her head around it—she didn't have to be the best at everything she did. Instead she could be her best in some things, the things she really liked. She understood that she had other reasons for trying new things, and having fun was moving up to the top of her list. Finally, Sally began to feel excited about trying soccer.

Chapter 10

Having Fun

Sally joined the soccer team and the season started a month later. Their coach taught them all sort of things like how to protect the ball from an opponent and how to dribble it down the field. One day when they were all feeling fearless, he taught them how to hit the ball with their heads. It was cool learning these new skills. When Sally played soccer she felt excited and carefree all at the same time. It was fun. It was one of her things. But for Sally, the best thing about being a Tiger was having fun with Jenny and all of her new friends—winning was the icing on the cake.

Over time the Tigers won some games and lost some games, as all teams do. Winning was way more fun, of course, but even when they lost it was okay. They still had fun and they were proud of themselves for playing hard. And mistakes were a normal part of things. Everyone made them. But with each mistake, the Tigers learned something new.

Spring days were growing longer and getting warmer and before they knew it, the Tigers were playing in their last game of the season. It was a bright sunny day. Yellow daffodils swayed gently in the breeze and the smell of freshly cut grass lingered in the air. Sally ran on to the field. In that moment she didn't have any worries…she felt happy. It wasn't the happiness that comes with reaching perfection. Nobody's perfect. It was the happiness that comes with having fun…the kind that comes from knowing that her best is enough…she is enough.